ISSUNBŌSHI

ISSUNBŌSHI

Illustrated by George Suyeoka
Adapted from the original folktales
by Robert B. Goodman and
Robert A. Spicer
Edited by Ruth Tabrah

AN ISLAND HERITAGE BOOK

Produced and published by Island Heritage Limited
Norfolk Island, Australia

For the Island Heritage distributor in your area,
please write or phone:

Island Heritage Limited (USA)
Editorial Offices
1020 Auahi St., Bldg. 3
Honolulu, Hawaii 96814
Phone: (808) 531-5091
Cable: HAWAIIBOOK

Engraving, printing, and binding by
Leefung - Asco Printers Ltd. Hong Kong

ISLAND HERITAGE

EDITORS
Robert B. Goodman
Robert A. Spicer

ASSOCIATE EDITOR
Carol A. Jenkins

CONSULTING EDITORS
Ruth Tabrah
Rubellite K. Johnson
Frances Kakugawa
George A. Fargo
Jodi Belknap

CONSULTING ART DIRECTORS
Yoshio Hayashi
Nella Hoffman
Herb Kawainui Kane

For my wife Irene,
and daughter Miya,
and my son Genn.

In the province of Settsu, in a village that is now Osaka, there once lived a couple who dreamed of a child of their own.

Year after year they climbed to the temple to ask the gods for a son.

The wife, Yaye, wanted a child so badly that one day she cried out: "I would be happy, o gods, for a boy-child even if he were no bigger than my thumb!"

O-kage-de! By the grace of the gods! Within that same month Yaye became pregnant. Together, she and her husband returned to the temple to give thanks for the child that was to come.

The day of the birth was joy - and astonishment!
"Yaye, the Gods listened well to you, woman! He is no
bigger than your thumb, indeed!

"Issunbōshi! One-inch boy. That is the name I give our son."

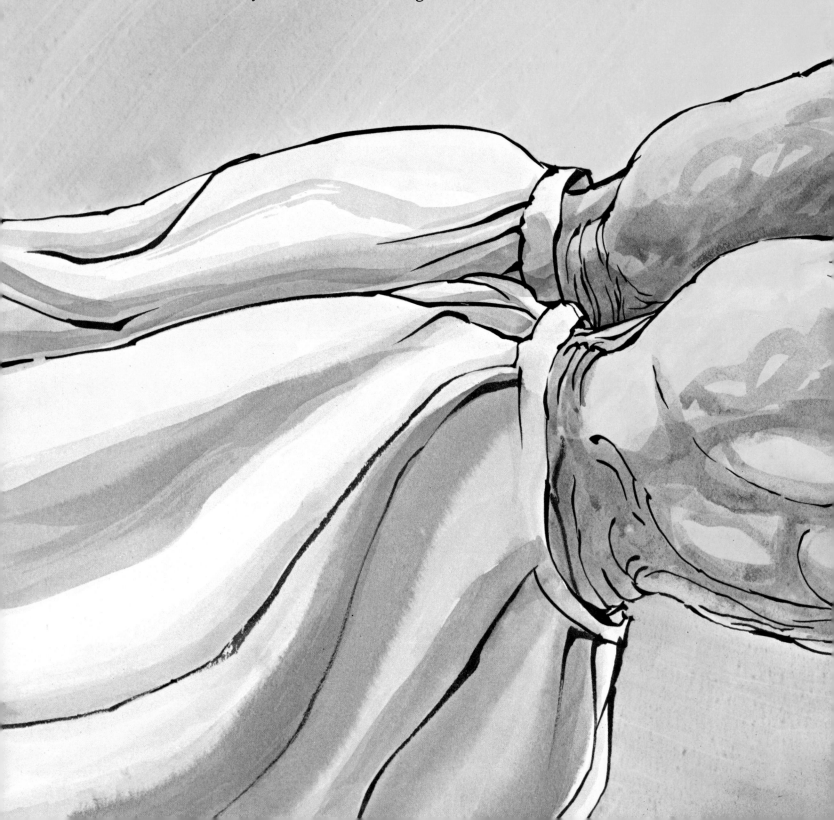

With loving patience they waited for the boy to grow bigger. He did not.

One grain of rice, a drop of tea, the tiniest fish was a feast for Issunbōshi.

Children came from all over the village to see him. They loved to play hide and seek and Issunbōshi always smiling and happy, always won.

He could hide anywhere. The children learned quickly to take care not to step on the little fellow. Everybody loved him.

"Oto-sama," said Issunbōshi, pointing up the river towards Kyoto, the city of the Emperor. "I will soon be sixteen. It is time for me to go out into the world. Give me permission to leave, father. I would like to serve in the house of a great lord."

His father nodded. "Our house will be lonely without you, my son. But it is true, you are sixteen. It is time to find your place as a man!"

"Come, Yaye, we must prepare our son for his journey."

There was much to do - food, weapons, clothing, and a boat were needed. A sewing needle became a sharp sword, hari-no-ken.

A soup bowl, owan, made a splendid boat, and hashi, a chopstick, was the oar.

His mother made a dumpling bag - mochi no fukuro - and filled it with food. She knew her son would be hungry on his journey.

"Make your fortune in the world with honor to the Emperor and to us," said the old man as he launched his son into the stream.

"Remember, your grandfather was once a vice-minister."

Yaye wiped away a mother's tears. "Genki-de!
Be careful!" she called. "Sayonara!"

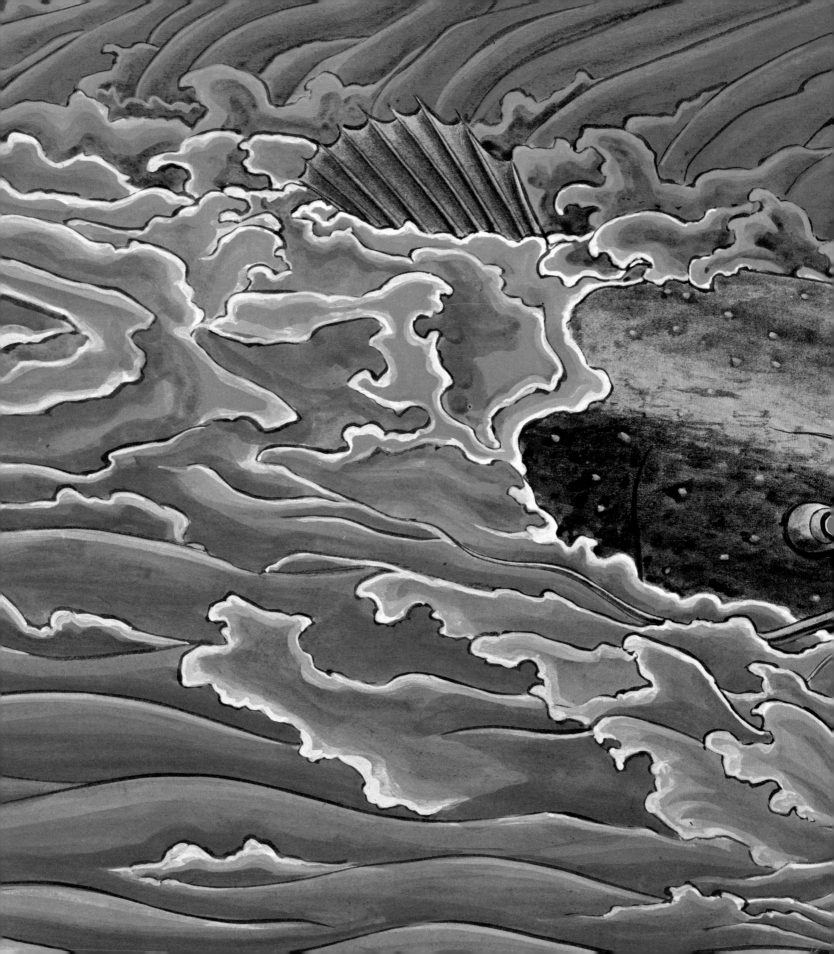

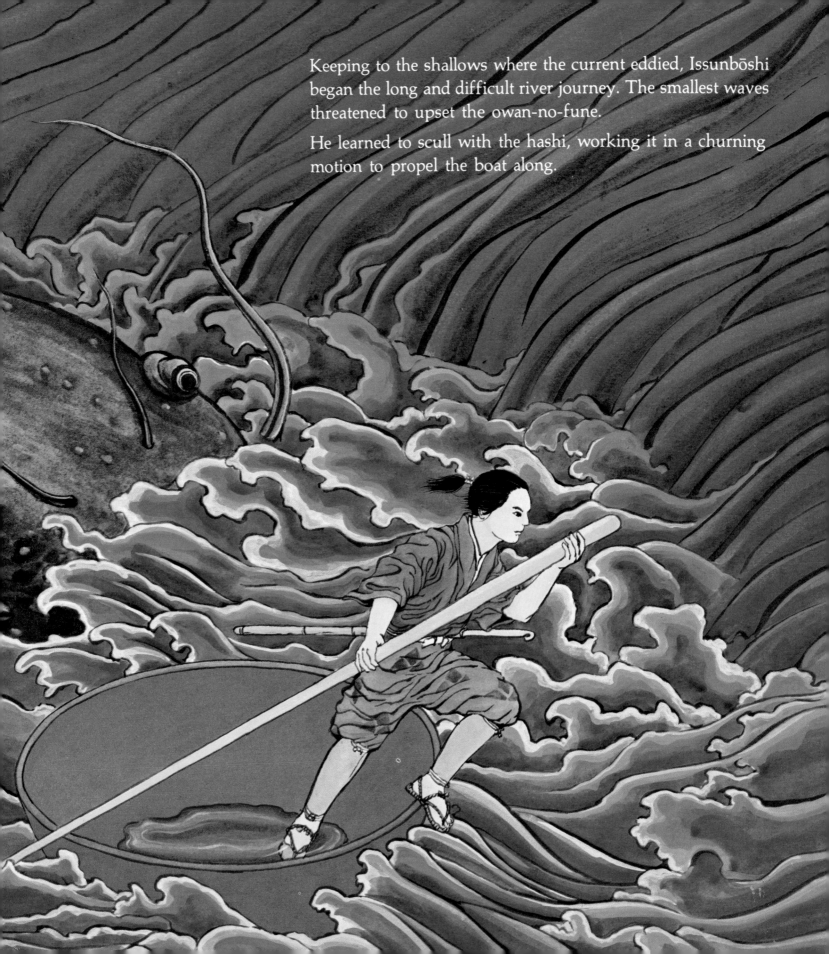

Keeping to the shallows where the current eddied, Issunbōshi began the long and difficult river journey. The smallest waves threatened to upset the owan-no-fune.

He learned to scull with the hashi, working it in a churning motion to propel the boat along.

A sudden rain shower filled him with panic. "The rain will fill my boat and I'll drown!" He sculled with all his might to get into the shelter of a lily pad.

The shower passed.

Issunbōshi was just casting off, when a giant frog, in search of insects, landed beside him with a great splash. The frog fixed his two great yellow eyes on the tiny warrior and prepared to swallow him.

Quick as a flash, Issunbōshi parried the darting tongue. The surprised frog stopped for a moment, then renewed his attack.

The boy fought with all his strength but he was no match for the giant frog.

The deadly tongue lashed out again and Issunbōshi felt himself being lifted into the air. He was certain that he would soon be inside the frog's gaping mouth.

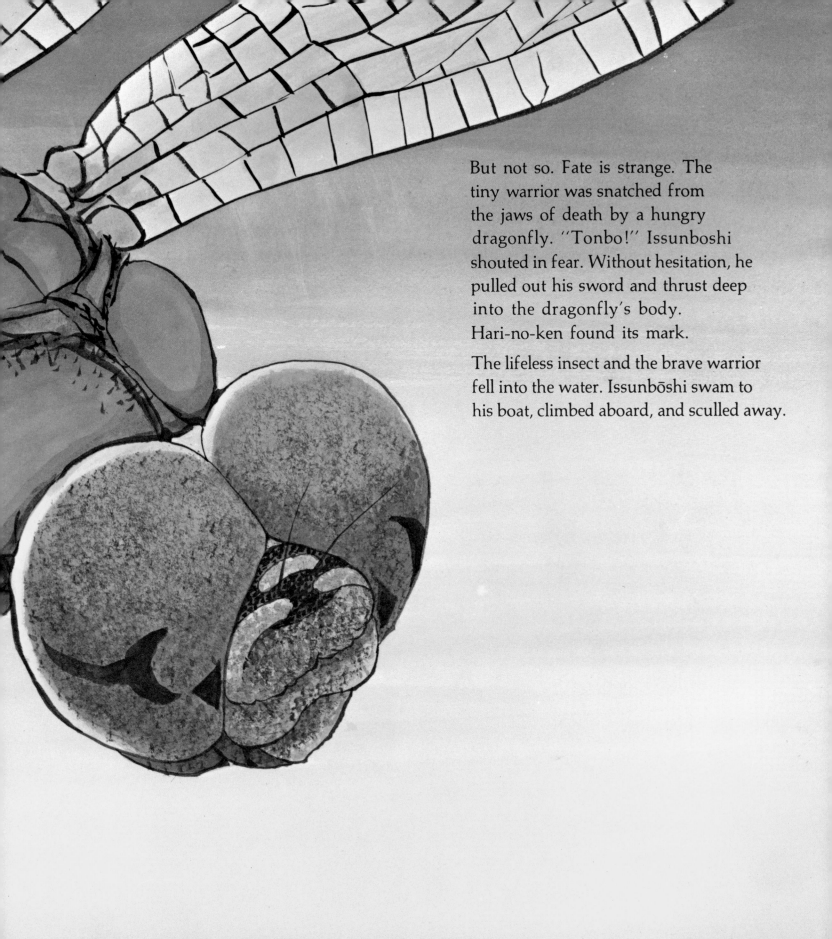

But not so. Fate is strange. The
tiny warrior was snatched from
the jaws of death by a hungry
dragonfly. "Tonbo!" Issunboshi
shouted in fear. Without hesitation, he
pulled out his sword and thrust deep
into the dragonfly's body.
Hari-no-ken found its mark.

The lifeless insect and the brave warrior
fell into the water. Issunbōshi swam to
his boat, climbed aboard, and sculled away.

Weary, sore, and hungry, after many days Issunbōshi sighted the temples and castle walls of the city of Kyoto.

No one noticed the tiny owan-no-fune on the busy surface of the river.

Issunbōshi found a landing place between two rocks. With hari-no-ken sheathed at his side, he clambered ashore.

Such traffic! Issunbōshi dodged for his life. How to find the house of a great lord in all this confusion?

"I must!" Issunbōshi resolved. "I will pledge my sword for a great lord's defense and honor. Then I can prove I'm a man and a brave fighter!"

"I will try this one!" thought Issunbōshi as he
finally stood before the gate of the
biggest house in the city.

He dusted his clothing, wiped the dirt from his
face, and stood proudly his full inch.

Late evening shadows were gathering as his
tiny bell-like voice called out, "Your
Lordship! I am Issunbōshi! I have come to offer
my services! Open your gate!"

Now it so happened that the Lord of the House was the Emperor's Prime Minister, a very sensitive man. Evening would find him in the garden listening to the insect symphony. Cicadas singing at sunset. Bees humming drowsily off for the night. This was the music that soothed him at the end of a day.

"What strange sound is that?" he wondered when he heard Issunbōshi calling.

He spoke to his attendant. "Open the gate carefully! I must see what that is!"

"I am Issunbōshi!" cried the young warrior.
"I have come to serve you. I am the grandson
of Horikawa!"

"Ah, so?" smiled the Prime Minister.
"That is a famous name, Horikawa-Sama.
And that is a fine sword you have, Issunbōshi. I like the sound of you! I accept
you into my service."

"Miyuki!" the Prime Minister called for
his daughter. "Here is your new bodyguard."

And so it was that Issunbōshi became a court favorite.
His friendly manner, his warm smile, and his fierce defense of
Miyuki won everyone's love and respect.
He accompanied her everywhere.

The Princess preferred Issunbōshi above all others. Affection grew between them as the seasons yielded - spring to summer, summer to the enchantment of the harvest moon.

For Issunbōshi it was also a difficult time. He was first a warrior pledged to protect her, yet his heart ached with love for the beautiful Miyuki. But how could he speak of love when he was hardly bigger than her thumb?

"Issunbōshi!" Miyuki's young voice called out one morning, "We must get ready. Today we must go to the Shrine at Ise."

For the first time the tiny warrior did not want to go along. He knew that this was the journey every young maiden must take. At the shrine, Miyuki would pray for a husband, a full-sized man.

Hiding his tears, Issunboshi led the Princess safely on the long journey to Ise.

But as Miyuki left the temple, two evil oni attacked without warning. Only Issunboshi whirled to face the monsters.
The other attendants fled in terror.

"Who are you?" laughed the oni. "A needle for a sword? Ha! I'll crush you with my little finger."

Issunbōshi seized his chance. "Ei!" he shouted.
His needle sharp sword plunged deep into the monster's eye.

Blinded, and bellowing with pain, the monster dropped
Issunbōshi and ran away.

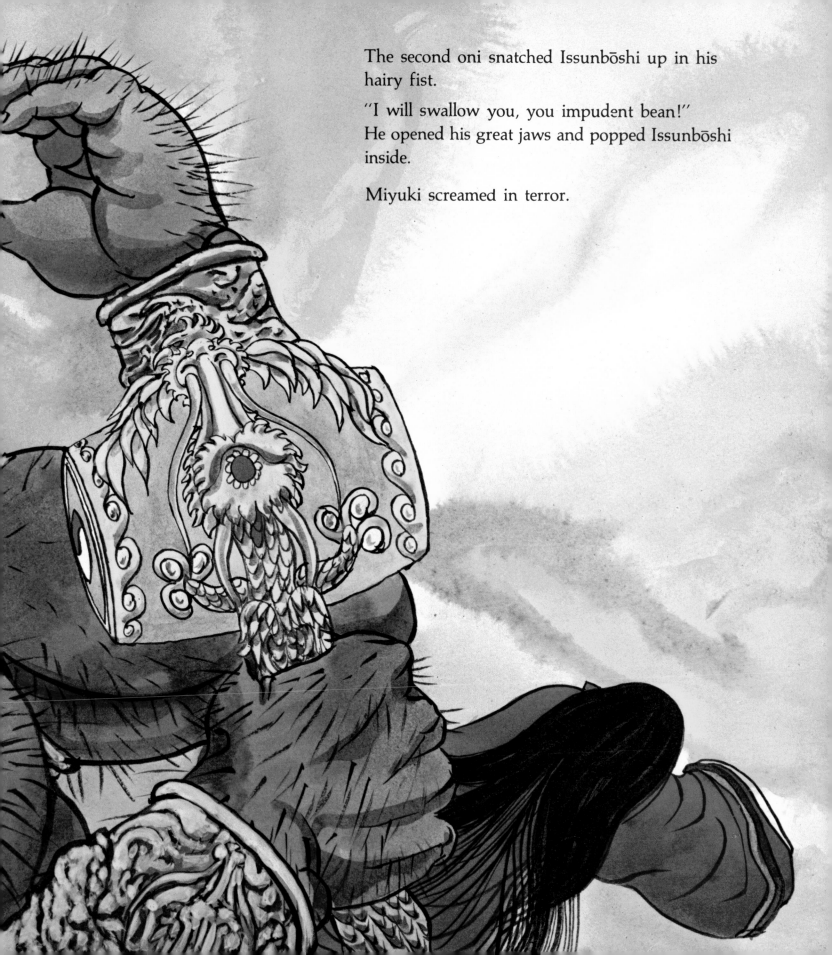

The second oni snatched Issunbōshi up in his hairy fist.

"I will swallow you, you impudent bean!" He opened his great jaws and popped Issunbōshi inside.

Miyuki screamed in terror.

Inside the monster's mouth, the tiny warrior dodged
the great teeth. Bracing himself, he buried hari-no-ken
deep in the monster's throat.

The oni coughed with a painful roar. Issunbōshi was
hurled out of the monster's mouth and landed in
the soft black hair of his beloved Miyuki.

Miyuki was overjoyed. Tenderly, she held Issunbōshi.

"I thought I would never see you again. I was so afraid and you were so brave!" Issunbōshi swelled with pride. He had proved his courage as a warrior.

"Look, Issunbōshi! The monsters dropped their magic mallet! If we strike it," said Miyuki, eagerly, "we can have any wish our hearts desire!

"Make a wish, my brave warrior!"

For Issunboshi, there was only one wish
- to be a full-sized man.

The mallet shimmered with a blinding golden light.
When they could see again - the Issunbōshi who
was no bigger than his father's thumb had
disappeared. In his place stood
a handsome young man.

The news traveled more quickly to
Kyoto than they did.

The Prime Minister came eagerly to greet them.
"Issunbōshi!", he exclaimed, "your new size
matches your courage!"

"My son, will you do me the great honor
of accepting my daughter as your bride?"

And so it was, Issunbōshi and his Princess were wed and lived happily ever after.

To this day, all over Japan, the story of Issunbōshi is famous. The inch-boy who had within himself the bravery, the determination, and the love that are the mark of every full-sized man.

An Introduction to Things Japanese

The Japanese objects
shown here are generally
vintage Heian to Muromachi
(700 a.d. to 1200 a.d.)

A. Red lacquered soup bowl, *Owan*
B. Iron sewing needle
C. Bamboo chopstick, *hashi*

D. Cart or carriage, ox drawn
E. Straw slippers
F. Aristocratic shoes of
leather and silk
G. Lacquered clogs
H. Kannon Bosatsu: Goddess
of mercy and benevolence

L. Oni, demon carrying his gold
and jewel-encrusted
jade magic hammer.

I. Wood lacquer inlay saddle
and gilt inlaid stirrups (metal)
J. Aristocratic hats (now primarily
K. the symbol of the emperor's headgear
and of Shinto Priests)

I

J   K   L

ISSUNBŌSHI

English version for the music by Judy and Masato Sato.

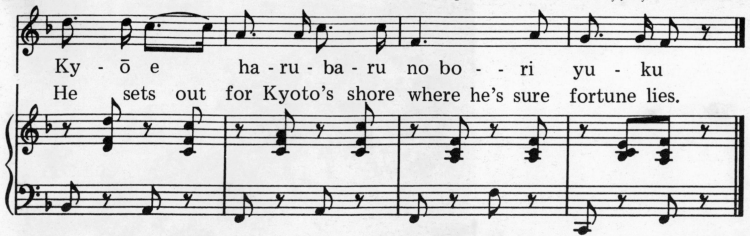

Ky - ō e ha - ru - ba - ru no bo - - ri yu - ku

He sets out for Kyoto's shore where he's sure fortune lies.

2. Kyō was Sanjō no daijin-dono ni
Kakaeraretaru Issunbōshi
Hōshi, Hōshi to okini-iri
Hime no otomo de kiyomizu e

3. Satemo kaeri no Kiyomizu-zaka ni
Oni ga ippiki araware idete
Kutte kakareba sono kuchi e
Hōshi tachimachi odorikomu

4. Hari no tachi oba sakate ni motte
Chikuri, chikuri to harajū tsukeba
Oni wa Hōshi o hakidashite
Isshōkenmei ni nigete yuku

5. Oni ga wasureta Uchide no Kozuchi
Uteba fushigi ya Issunbōshi
Hito uchi goto ni sei ga nobite
Ima wa rippana ō - otoko

2. Long and hard was his trip to Kyoto City,
"At your service, my lord, I am Issunbōshi,"
cried the small warrior at the great lord's gate.
"I will surely serve you well!" said Issunbōshi.

3. Off they go to the temple on the mountain
Princess, daughter of the lord, and Issunbōshi
From the shadows there sprang an oni fierce,
Issunbōshi jumped into his mouth.

4. Hari no tachi was his trusty blade.
Stabbing, jabbing in the oni's stomach did he fight, and then
Screeching, yelling, the oni spit him out,
Running, howling, the oni ran from him.

5. Left behind on the ground, a magic mallet.
"Hurry, hurry, make your wish now, Issunbōshi!"
Came a blinding flash and when it was gone,
Issunbōshi was a full grown man.

Fukaku Kansha-shimafu

Island Heritage is grateful to
Fumiyo Anematsu, Dr. Hiroko Ikeda,
Keiko Takeuchi, and Judy and Masato
Sato for their contributions to Issunbōshi.

We also wish to thank Edward R. Bendet,
and Martin I. Rosenberg. Special
thanks go to Mr. and Mrs. Paul Slavey,
Ron Gandee, Robert Lee, Penny McCracken
and Elizabeth Owen of Pacific Phototype, Inc.